Dear Parents and Educators,

Welcome to Penguin Young Readers! A[s you may] know that each child develops at his o[wn pace, in] speech, critical thinking, and, of course, reading. Penguin Young Readers recognizes this fact. As a result, each Penguin Young Readers book is assigned a traditional easy-to-read level (1–4) as well as a Guided Reading Level (A–P). Both of these systems will help you choose the right book for your child. Please refer to the back of each book for specific leveling information. Penguin Young Readers features esteemed authors and illustrators, stories about favorite characters, fascinating nonfiction, and more!

Max & Ruby™: Ruby's Tea Party

LEVEL 2

GUIDED READING LEVEL **G**

This book is perfect for a **Progressing Reader** who:
- can figure out unknown words by using picture and context clues;
- can recognize beginning, middle, and ending sounds;
- can make and confirm predictions about what will happen in the text; and
- can distinguish between fiction and nonfiction.

Here are some **activities** you can do during and after reading this book:
- Compound Words: A compound word is made when two words are joined together to form a new word. There are several compound words in this story. On a piece of paper, copy these two columns of words:

table	bath
out	glass
spy	cloth
bird	side

Then have the child draw a line from a word in the first column to a word in the second column to create a compound word.
- Make Connections: In this story, Max pretends that napkins are pirate ships and a jewelry box is a treasure chest. Talk about a time you played with objects in your house and imagined they were something else.

Remember, sharing the love of reading with a child is the best gift you can give!

—Bonnie Bader, EdM
  Penguin Young Readers program

*Penguin Young Readers are leveled by independent reviewers applying the standards developed by Irene Fountas and Gay Su Pinnell in *Matching Books to Readers: Using Leveled Books in Guided Reading*, Heinemann, 1999.

PENGUIN YOUNG READERS
An Imprint of Penguin Random House LLC

All artwork from the series *Max & Ruby* used under license from Nelvana Limited. Max & Ruby
(Episodes 1–26): © 2002–2003 Nelvana Limited. All rights reserved.

Max & Ruby © Rosemary Wells. Licensed by Nelvana Limited. NELVANA is a registered trademark
of Nelvana Limited. CORUS is a trademark of Corus Entertainment Inc. All rights reserved.
Published in 2016 by Penguin Young Readers, an imprint of Penguin Random House LLC,
345 Hudson Street, New York, New York 10014. Manufactured in China.

ISBN 978-1-101-99507-5   10 9 8 7 6 5 4 3 2 1

Max & Ruby™

Ruby's Tea Party

Penguin Young Readers
An Imprint of Penguin Random House

Ruby is having a tea party.

Max is playing pirate.

"Max, can you put this
tablecloth on the table
for my tea party?" says Ruby.
"Arr!" says Max.

Max takes the tablecloth.

But he doesn't put it on the table.

He makes a sail

for his pirate ship!

Ruby comes outside

with snacks.

But there's no tablecloth

on the table!

"Max, the tablecloth is

for the table,

not for a pirate sail!"

says Ruby.

Ruby puts the tablecloth

on the table.

She puts the snacks

on the table, too.

Her dolls sit in chairs

around the table.

Ruby folds napkins

for her tea party.

"Arr!" says Max.

"I can't play pirate, Max.

I'm having a tea party!"

says Ruby.

"Can you please put these

napkins on the table?"

Max wants to play pirate.

He puts the napkins

in the birdbath.

They are pirate ships!

"Max, these napkins are not

pirate ships," says Ruby.

"They are for my tea party!"

Ruby puts the napkins

on the table.

Her tea party is almost ready!

Max looks through his

pirate spyglass.

"Arr!" he says.

Ruby has cakes

for her tea party.

But her dolls are not

in their chairs!

Oh no! Where are they?

Max is playing pirate

with Ruby's dolls.

"Arr!" says Max.

"Max, you can't play pirate
with my dolls!
I'm having a tea party,"
says Ruby.

"Can you put my dolls back

on the chairs, Max?"

says Ruby.

"I'm going to put on a new

outfit for my tea party."

Ruby puts on a dress with a bow

for her tea party.

"Now I need to put on
my necklace," says Ruby.

But Ruby can't find

her necklace.

Her jewelry box is gone, too!

Ruby has an idea.

"Max, let's play pirate!"

says Ruby.

"Let's dig for

buried pirate treasure!"

"Arr!" says Max.

Max brings Ruby

to the garden.

"Is this where we look for

buried treasure?" asks Ruby.

"Arr!" says Max.

Max starts to dig.

"I think we found

our treasure!" says Ruby.

"Treasure chest!" says Max.

The treasure chest is

Ruby's jewelry box.

"Look, my necklace!"

says Ruby.

"I'm going to wear it

to my tea party.

Will Pirate Max be my

special guest?" asks Ruby.

"Arr!" says Max.